This book belongs to

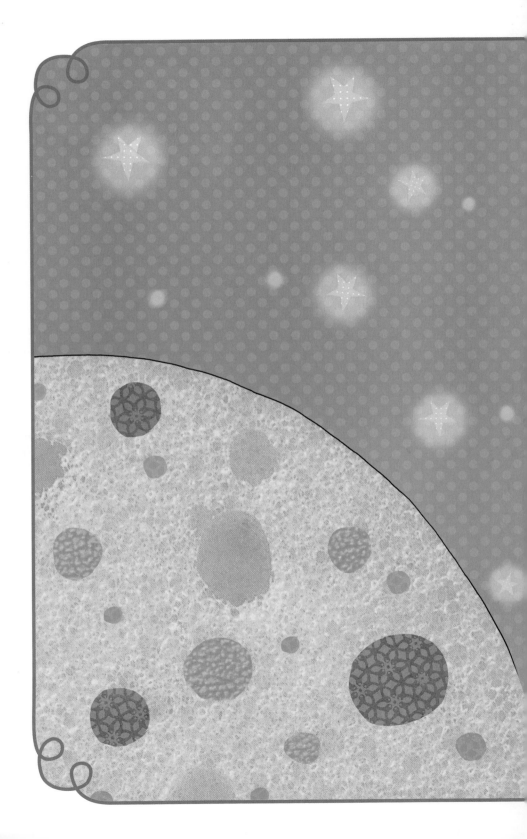

Lola the Lollipop Fairy

Good-bye Moon, See You Soon!

Other books in the series:

Big Top Bother

Lola's Lollipopper Showstopper

Lola's Lollipop Shop

Copyright © 2014 make believe ideas ltd
The Wilderness, Berkhamsted, Hertfordshire, HP4 2AZ, UK.
501 Nelson Place, P.O. Box 141000, Nashville, TN 37214-1000, USA.

www.makebelieveideas.com

Reading together

This book is designed to be fun for children who are just starting to read on their own. They will enjoy and benefit from some time discussing the story with an adult. Encourage them to pause and talk about what is happening in the pictures. Help them to spot familiar words and sound out the letters in harder words. Look at the following ways you can help your child take those first steps in reading:

Explore the story

Make the most of each page by talking about the pictures and spotting key words. Encourage your child to sound out the letters in any words he or she does not know. Look at the common "key" words listed at the back of the book and see which of them your child can find on each page.

Test understanding

It is one thing to understand one word at a time, but it is important to make sure your child can understand the story as a whole!

Ask your child questions as you read the story, for example:

- Do you like the aliens?
- Where does Lola go?
- What do the aliens give Lola?
- Play "find the obvious mistake." Read the text as your child looks at the words with you, but make an obvious mistake to see if he or she catches it. Ask your child to correct you and provide the right word.

Activity section

A "Ready to tell" section at the end of the book encourages children to remember what happened in the story and then retell it. A picture dictionary page helps children to increase their vocabulary, and a useful word page reinforces their knowledge of the most common words. There is also a practical activity inspired by the story and a "Lola and her friends" section where children can learn about all of Lola the Lollipop Fairy's friends!

Lola is ready to fly to
the moon. She puts on
her glasses and circus hat.

Lola waves good-bye
to her pet cat, Jaffa.

She zooms up
into the sky.

"The moon looks like a big lollipop!" says Lola.

There are aliens on the moon.
They are small and green.

13

Lola plays and dances
with the aliens all day.
"I wish I could stay,"
says Lola.

It is nearly six o'clock!
Lola has to get home for
her special circus show.

18

"Please take this special lollipop as a gift from us," say the aliens.
"Thank you," says Lola.

Lola flies back home.
"Good-bye, Moon,"
says Lola. "See you soon!"

Ready to tell

Can you remember what happened in the story? Look at each picture and try retelling the story.

1

2

3

4

5

6

7

Lola's fairy dictionary

alien

dance

cat

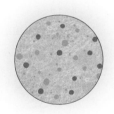

moon

fly

lollipop

Lola's useful words

Here are some key words used in context. Make simple sentences for the other words in the border.

Lola goes **to** the moon.

The moon looks **like** a big lollipop.

Lola and the aliens like to **play**.

The aliens are very friendly.

The aliens give Lola **this** lollipop.

Lola and her friends

Lola is in charge of the circus show. Lola likes to think of new ideas, such as her lollipop shop! Linda and Lulu are her sisters.

Linda performs in the circus show with Lulu and Lola. Linda is a weight lifter. She also likes to sing and dance!

Lulu spins plates in the circus show. Sometimes she juggles lollipops too!

Jaffa is the circus cat. He likes to join in with the shows. Sometimes he wears a hat, just like Lola.

Morris the mouse is Jaffa's best friend. He is very nosy! Morris likes to know what is going on at all times.

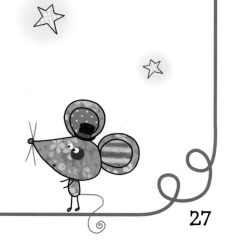

Lisa is Lola's friend and she loves lollipops! Sometimes she performs exciting tricks in Lola's circus show.

Lara is Linda's friend. She performs on the flying trapeze at Lola's circus. She is very good at it!

Lily is Lisa's sister.
She loves lollipops too!
Lily's favorite lollipop
flavor is lemon.

Lexi, Lulu's friend,
loves the circus show.
She likes Lola's cannon
ride the best, and would
really like to have a go!

Moon mobile

Make your own moon
to hang in your room.

You will need:

- 1 sheet of cardboard
- marker pen or pencil
- scissors
- hole-punch
- string
- pens, glitter, and
  sparkly decorations
- sticky tack or tape

What to do:

1. First, draw the moon in a shape of your choice – round or crescent-shaped.

2. Ask a grown-up to help you cut around your drawing.

3. Next, use a hole-punch to make a hole at the top of your moon.

4. Cut a piece of string long enough to hang the moon up. Push this through the hole and tie it.

5. Finally, decorate your moon any way you like. Lola thinks the moon looks like a lollipop. What will yours look like? You can make some extra star decorations in the same way.

6. When it is all finished, ask a grown-up to stick it with tack or tape to the ceiling of your room. Now you have your very own moon mobile!